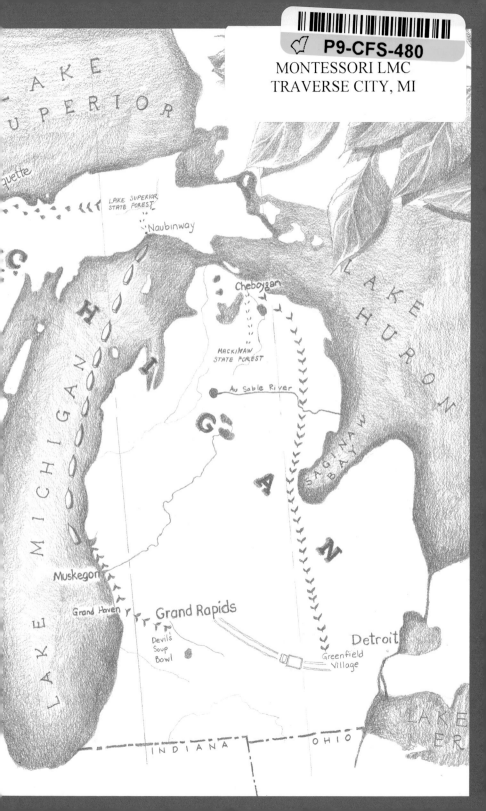

LAKE
SUPERIOR

quette

LAKE SUPERIOR
STATE FOREST

Naubinway

C

H

I

Cheboygan

MACKINAW
STATE FOREST

Au Sable River

G

A

N

L A K E
H U R O N

SAGINAW
BAY

LAKE MICHIGAN

Muskegon

Grand Haven

Grand Rapids

Devil's
Soup
Bowl

Detroit

Greenfield
Village

INDIANA

OHIO

LAKE
ER

Mitt, the Michigan Mouse

by
Kathy-jo Wargin

illustrated by
Karen Busch Holman

mitten press

All inquiries should be addressed to:

Mitten Press

An imprint of Ann Arbor Media Group LLC

2500 S. State Street

Ann Arbor, MI 48104

Printed and bound by Edwards Brothers, Ann Arbor, Michigan, USA.

10   9   8   7   6   5   4   3   2   1

Library of Congress Cataloging-in-Publication Data on file.

ISBN 13: 978-1-58726-303-3

ISBN 10: 1-58726-303-3

Book design by Somberg Design

www.sombergdesign.com

Contents

CHAPTER ONE

The Mitten

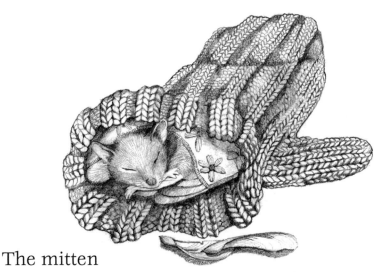

The mitten was the only home the mouse had ever known. It was made of thick red wool and hidden in a fallen white spruce tree deep in the woods of northern Michigan. The spruce had toppled in a storm years before, and time had worn it hollow. The mitten was tucked inside, where it stayed dry when the forest was soaked with summer rain. It kept Mitt warm and cozy when winter winds came howling through the tall pine trees, shaking down cones and needles on snowy nights. And although the mitten was small, it was just the right size for a white-footed mouse named Mitt.

His nest inside the mitten was made from red-breasted nuthatch feathers, and his pillow was a velvety-white pussy willow bud. His blanket was an old piece of handkerchief found near the riverbed, and Mitt liked the yellow daisies sewn around its edge.

Mitt lived alone with no mother or father or sisters or brothers. He had them at one time, but now had only memories. The memories he had, though small and distant, were pleasant ones. He remembered that when he was born, he had no

fur and couldn't see, and so his mother
kept him warm and fed. And every night,
she would gently rock him in the moon-
shaped milkweed pod that was his cradle.

Sometimes, when Mitt was almost asleep
and his mind went drifting, he could hear

his mother singing to him. And though he saw nothing more than a shadow of her face in his dreams, he could still feel her huddling in with him and his brothers and sisters. From this he remembered that her kisses were soft and warm, and her breath was sweeter than apple spice pie.

It always bothered Mitt that he never knew what happened to his mother and father and brothers and sisters. As it is in most mice families, it just happened to be that one morning he woke up alone and on his own.

The Party

Mitt rose to the noisy chatter of red squirrels and the sharp, cawing sound of common crows. Most everyone in the forest was getting ready for Inger's birthday party, and Mitt was happy to be invited. Inger, a sweet porcupine pup, was now four months old and nearly ready to go out on her own. Mitt worked neatly to wrap a stack of sugar maple seeds he collected from the forest floor. It was a lovely autumn morning, and he had found many seeds. He made the pile by carefully placing one seed on top of the other until he could tie a bow around them out of a long piece of field grass. Inger was fond of sugar maple seeds, and Mitt was fond of Inger.

Mitt left the red wool mitten and hurried along the runways he and other forest mice had made. Their paths crisscrossed through the woods, passing under logs and over mossy clumps. They burrowed into hidden tunnels beneath open grassy spots, and went under the earth where the soil was sandy and light. As he raced along, it did not take him long before he was at the shallow end of the stream. Mitt knew the stream well, and across it was the falling-down cabin where Inger and her family lived.

Mitt stepped inside to say hello to Inger in the quiet way that a mouse should do. But before he had a chance to do so, CRASH! Mitt was slammed from behind so hard he went topsy-turvy into a nearby pile of wood chips. When he fell, his lovely gift of seeds went scattering all across the floor. It was Berg! Berg had pushed Mitt out of the way and stepped up to Inger, handing her a small silver coin, much to Inger's delight. Berg, a bushy-tailed wood rat from Cheboygan, collected shiny things and was trying very hard to impress Inger with his gift.

But Mitt was not impressed. Berg was always pushing and shoving or boasting about his treasures. Now Mitt had no gift for Inger.

The guests arrived in many woodland ways. A family of minks slipped through the window, cheeping about their journey

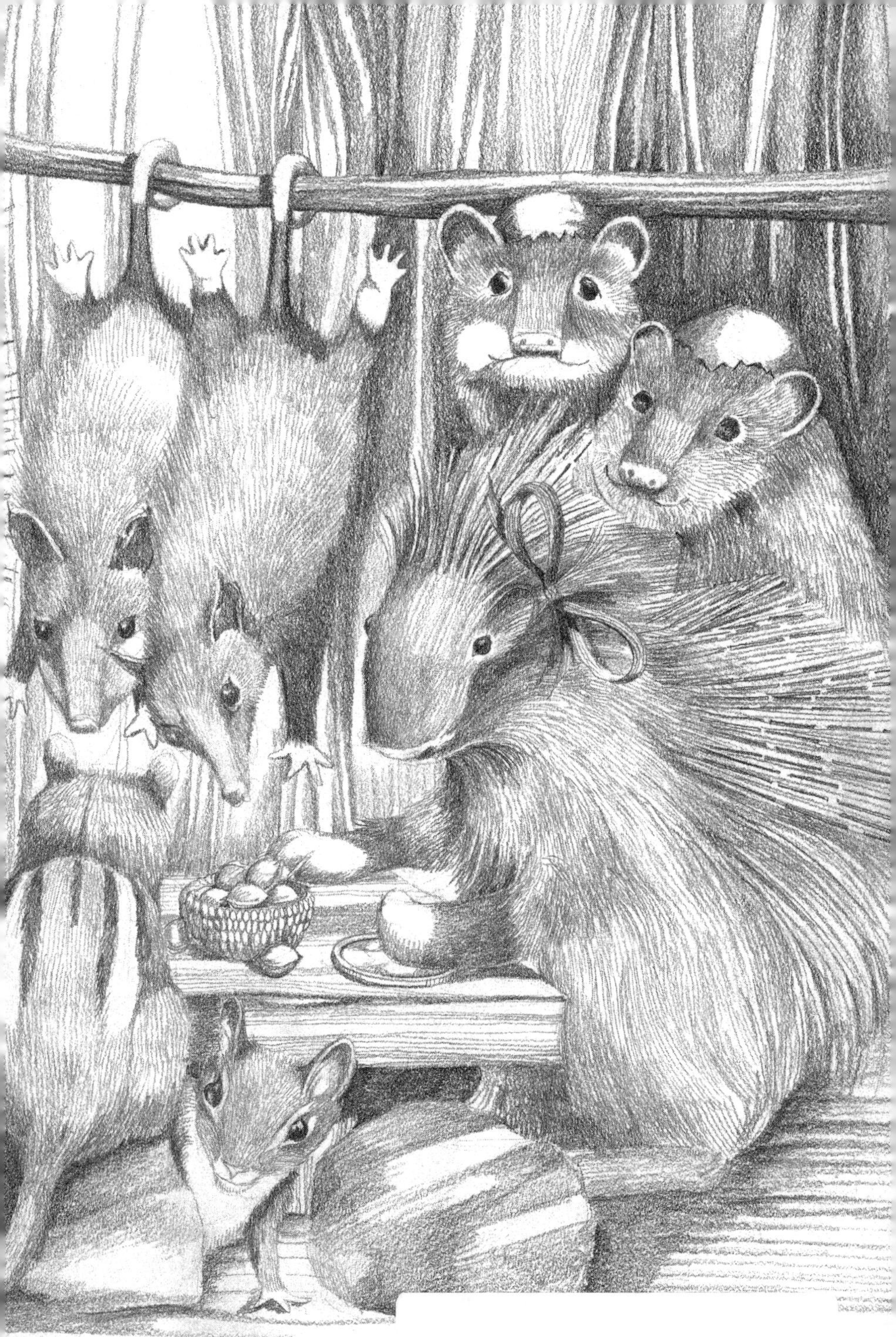

from the riverbank, while three eastern chipmunks scampered through the doorway chirping on about a red fox that had been chasing them. There was an opossum with five kits on her back, three long-tailed weasels, and a family of common raccoons. When nearly all had arrived, Inger's mother told each guest to have a seat at the table and put on their party hats. Mitt liked party hats, and his was made from an old empty acorn shell. The raccoon, Grima, was given a hat made from an empty bird nest, and the mink family wore hats made from broken robin eggs. But Berg, the bushy-tailed wood rat, would not wear his hat because it was made from an old ice-cream cone and he thought he was much too important to wear something so silly.

As the animals exchanged stories in the way that animals do, the porcupines brought out the food. What a wonderful feast it would be! Mitt watched as the table was filled with trumpet mushrooms, fairy butter, brownie caps, and stinkhorns. There were black cherry pits for nibbling and cattail tops for chewing, and even an empty forest snail shell filled with dew for sipping.

Mitt enjoyed the treats very much. He laughed and smiled and played jumping games with his friends. But back at home, things were about to change.

CHAPTER THREE
Digby

The animals that remained home from the party sounded their alarm in the usual way. There was chirping and whistling, peeping and buzzing. They spotted an intruder up the trail, but could not see with any certainty who or what it was. A pair of northern flying squirrels flew from tree to tree, trying to catch a glimpse of the monster. When they got close enough, they clicked and chucked their description to the other animals. Word quickly spread through the forest by way of trees and thickets, telling how it was tall and gray and fast and shaggy. The lummox, they exclaimed, was BIG! And it was coming their way.

The gray dog was an Irish wolfhound named Digby, and he looked more like a small pony with a beard than he did a dog. His legs were long and thin like spindles, and they carried him in a gallop that went more side-to-side than forward. His beard was filled with thistles and bristles and brambles, and his feet made a dull flumping sound as he scrambled through the forest nosing wintergreen and northern dewberry. To the boy Jack, Digby was the finest dog ever.

The pair was heading to the
stream, which was not far from
the hollowed out tree where

Mitt's home was safely tucked. The stream was clear and shallow, wide and slow-moving. Fallen logs and sticks and branches cluttered its flow, while clumps of moss gathered around the turned-up tree roots that lined the banks. Jack climbed up a large mound of moss to touch its soft green clusters when Boom! Digby leaped upon the mound too, knocking Jack straight into the stream where he found himself fixed in muck. His rubber boots slurped through the water, sucking through the cold, thick mud with each step. Jack was trying to make his way back to the dry banks of the forest stream when Digby came splashing by, getting him wetter still. Digby then went galloping from tree to tree, sniffing and snorting and woofing and huffing, picking up leaves and sticks only to toss them aside.

Feeling betrayed by Digby and his lack of concern about tossing him into the water, Jack decided it was time to go home.

Digby followed, but then caught a scent that made him curious. He raised his brow and pricked his ears, then stuck his nose inside a dense thicket of wood ferns covering a fallen spruce tree. He poked around and grabbed the small mitten he found inside. Then he ran away.

CHAPTER FOUR
The Joke

Mitt felt sad that his
gift for Inger had been
ruined. Thinking about
how to better the situation, Mitt decided to
tell Inger a joke for her birthday gift
instead. He thought it might impress her,
but he wasn't entirely sure. So he leaned
over to brothers Bertel and Bengt, two very

jolly deer mice with eyes much too large for their heads, and whispered, "What do you get when you cross a goat with an owl?" The brothers looked at him as if they hadn't a clue, and so with perfect pause Mitt proclaimed loudly, "a hootin' nanny!" Bertel and Bengt fell to the floor laughing in the way that tiny mice do, and this gave Mitt the courage to tell Inger the joke. It wasn't a stack of sugar maple seeds, but it was something.

What Mitt hadn't noticed was that Berg had been hiding in the corner eavesdropping. Moments later, everybody was called together for Inger's birthday cake, which was a very large mushroom cap with old summer blueberries. Should he tell the joke now, he thought? Mitt took his tiny

mouse paw and groomed his top hairs. He hedged back and forth a bit. He held his tail in his right paw and scratched his chin with his left. Then finally, thinking the moment was just right, Mitt began to speak. But before he could utter the first word, Berg the wood rat broke in and hollered out, "Say Inger, what do you get when you cross an owl with a goat?"

From there, Berg told the whole joke and while everybody was laughing including Inger, Mitt took off his little acorn hat and slipped away from the cabin. It was time to go home.

CHAPTER FIVE

Mitt's Return

"Help, help! Help me, my mitten is gone!"
cried Mitt. Mitt's dear friend Lempi, an elk
calf, was the first to arrive. It was well past
dark and she had been out in the forest

eating the last grasses
and twigs of autumn. "It's gone, it's gone!
My mitten is gone! Oh, no, where could it
be? My warm cozy house is gone!"

Mitt flew into a frenzy of worry and began
to drum his forefeet on the dry fallen
leaves. Lempi nosed around some to see if

perhaps the wind had blown it out of place, or deeper into the forest. A little brown bat came swooping in and settled on the lowest branch.

"It was that boy," said the little brown bat. "I heard it from the red flying squirrels. It was that little boy Jack and his great big dog." Mitt knew of Jack and Digby. He knew they came through the woods often, and that they lived in Cheboygan where there were houses and cars and boats and all sorts of dangers for a mouse.

"Mitt," said a chorus of voices, for by now three meadow voles, a masked shrew, and a black-capped chickadee had joined them. "Mitt, we can help you make a new home. We will find a new log and make you a new bed and everything!"

Meanwhile, a family of ovenbirds began searching frantically, kicking up the forest floor with their long beaks. "Nothing here!" they pipped. "Nothing here, nothing here!"

Mitt had no mother or father or sisters or brothers. The mitten was all he had left and now it was gone. At this, Mitt knew exactly what he needed to do. And so he left.

CHAPTER SIX
Butterball

Mitt thought all
he had to do
was get to
Cheboygan and find out
where Jack lived and ask for his mitten
back. Simple enough. *Or so he thought.*

It took him two weeks to run through the
forest to the edge of Cheboygan. Once he

arrived, he followed the riverbank to the center of town. He scurried past the factory and the stores until he came to a neighborhood of small houses, large houses, bright houses, old houses. But where did Jack and Digby live? Mitt went along the street, but stopped to gnaw on some black walnuts he found nearby. And that's where it happened.

The cat came out of nowhere; its fur was tangled and matted. It was big around the middle and the color of an orange that had stayed in the sun three days too long. The cat had a black eye patch tied around its head and two bottom teeth poking up and outward like tiny swords. Mitt thought that perhaps such a cat would have a name like Sid or Spike or Scratch.

Mitt tried to hide in a huge pile of freshly raked leaves. As soon as he dashed inside, the wind began to blow sending the leaves this way and that. His cover was blown! There was no place to go! Looking from side to side, Mitt ran beneath the first dense shrub he could find. The rosebush poked and pricked and needled him nearly to shreds, but even so, he managed to stay still. The wind began to rise again, pushing the thorny rose stems back and forth with each gust. One big thorn was blown upwards, catching Mitt right in the rear and sending him flying into the oncoming steps of the big orange cat. And then everything went dark.

"Boo," said the cat, pushing Mitt to the ground. His voice was deep and low, and he spoke slow and mean-like. Mitt looked into the cat's eye and felt a shiver of fear.

Mitt did the only thing he could think to do. He spoke. "I'm looking for a dog," he said, "a great big dog."

"Aren't we all," smirked the cat, whose two shiny teeth looked much larger and sharper up close. But Mitt was not going to give up that quickly. "I'm looking for a dog," said Mitt once more, "he's big and clumsy."

"Oh that narrows it down," said the smug cat. Mitt squirmed a bit to the left and then the right before taking a deep breath. "The dog has a beard. And a boy named Jack."

The cat pushed his paw down a bit harder and then stuck his big fat nose up to Mitt.

"Hey mousie, look at me. I'm a mousetrap!" said the cat.

This time, Mitt thought fast. "Knock knock," he said.

"Who's there?" asked the cat.

"Detail," said Mitt.

"Detail who?" the cat responded.

"Detail is de back end of the cat!" With that, the cat began to laugh and, without meaning to, lost his hold on Mitt. This gave Mitt just enough wiggle room to make a break for the cat's tail. He grabbed it quickly and hung on with all his might. The cat ran to and fro, back and forth, yet Mitt held tight. Then he crawled up the cat's back to sit on his head, just out of his reach.

At that, Mitt asked, "So what's your name anyway, tough guy?"

The cat was ashamed of his name and could barely choke the word out. But he did. "Butterball," he said in a voice so quiet Mitt could barely hear him. "My name is Butterball."

CHAPTER SEVEN
The Windowsill

Butterball knew where Digby and Jack lived.

He had known it all along, for a good cat knows the home of each dog. And so, the pair scrambled down Bailey Street to a bright blue house with white trim and yellow shutters. There was a short white picket fence all the way around, and an arbor above the entrance to the sidewalk with a sign that read McGreevy.

But there was no sign of a dog. There was no sign of a boy. It was getting late so Butterball dropped Mitt off near the gate.

"Are you sure this is it?" Mitt asked again. But Butterball didn't answer Mitt's question. He simply walked away, leaving Mitt all by himself. It was going to be a long night.

Mitt watched the house for signs of Digby or Jack. But there were none. Mitt was growing weary. He wondered if perhaps he should just go back to the forest. But something inside told Mitt to wait. And so he did.

Mitt grabbed a piece of wasp nest blowing by and rolled it around his shoulders to keep warm. He waited. He watched. And then it happened.

One by one, two lights turned on in the McGreevy home. Mitt saw through a small window a mother, a father, and a boy eating dinner. Oh, how hungry Mitt was! How he wanted nothing more than a thick slice of hard cheese with black cherry pits. He waited and watched. They were laughing and smiling at each other, and Mitt couldn't help but wonder what his own mother was doing right then. When they finished, Mitt saw the boy leave. A light flickered on in the upstairs window. Mitt wanted to see where the boy was going, so in the dark of night, he climbed an oak tree growing next to the house. He went little by little, branch by branch, carefully balancing every step with his tail. It didn't take long before Mitt was directly across from the window, and staring inside.

He could see it! His mitten was lying on the windowsill in the boy's room and he could see it!

CHAPTER EIGHT

Mitt Speaks

Tap! Tap! Tap! The tapping started early that morning. Tap! Tap! Tap! It sounded like a coin or a pencil or a sparrow beak tapping upon the glass. Jack was still sleepy when he went to the window. The young boy had to wipe his eyes in disbelief when he saw a little mouse pounding on his window with a balled up paw.

"You have my mitten!" cried Mitt.

Jack, not understanding the mouse, pressed his nose to the glass and strained to hear.

"I see you have my mitten and I would very much like to have it back."

But still, Jack could not hear what the mouse was saying and the mouse was losing his patience. It was not easy for Mitt to be so close to his mitten and unable to have it. Noticing this, Jack McGreevy did the only proper thing he could think to do. He opened the window and invited the mouse inside.

Mitt rushed inside and breathed, "Thank you, thank you! Thank you so much, I thought I would be standing out there forever."

Jack smiled at the little mouse and put out his hand. He had always wanted a pet mouse, but his mother told him that having a dog like Digby was punishment enough for any family. As well, his mother wasn't fond of mice, or frogs or spiders or

anything else that wiggled or squirmed. But that didn't matter to Jack. He was thrilled to have a mouse in his bedroom. And Jack, who was able to understand a bit of what Mitt was trying to say in the funny way that mice will say it, spoke back to Mitt.

"You say this is your mitten?" he asked.

Mitt replied, "Yes, it is my mitten and I would very much like it back."

But Jack wasn't so sure he wanted to give it back. He was using it. He had made a camp for his toy soldier on the windowsill, and he was using the mitten for a sleep-sack. It was just the right size, and he had always wanted his soldier to have a wool sleep-sack.

Jack picked up the soldier in the mitten and uttered to Mitt, "Well, why do you want it back?"

At first Mitt didn't want to tell Jack about his mother or father. He wasn't sure that a young boy would understand how it felt not to have parents, or how the mitten was all he had.

But Mitt saw no other way, and so hopped onto Jack's pillow and told the story about how his mother had rocked him in a cradle made from a milkweed pod. He told how they had lived in a nice large spruce tree, and how she sang sweet songs to him while his father fed him small milk-white berries. He told about his many brothers and sisters and how it just happened to be that one day, he woke up all alone.

After listening, Jack decided he didn't need the mitten as much as Mitt did, and said, "Well that would be fine, I guess. I couldn't imagine not having my mother or father."

"Say," said Jack, getting a new idea, "why don't you live here with me? You can sleep in your mitten and I will bring you good

things to eat every
day. You will be safe and warm and we can
play together after school."

Mitt thought for a moment before speaking. "It sounds rather perfect, is there a catch?" asked Mitt.

"Well, I guess there's a catch," said Jack.

"What is it then?"

"Well, if my mother sees you, *you're dead.*"

Mitt knew right away he was better off in the woods. He explained to Jack how nice the forest was, how he loved sweet-gale thickets and raspberry bushes. He told how he loved climbing the black spruces and white pines to snatch the best cone seeds. He told him about his friends Lempi and Inger, and the deer mice Bertel and Bengt. Jack listened closely.

"Well then," he said, "instead of you living here, I will visit you there."

Right then, the boy's mother called Jack downstairs for breakfast. Jack left, and Mitt sat alone on the bed, wondering how to get his mitten out of the house. But a solution was nowhere in sight.

CHAPTER NINE

Digby's Romp

Jack returned and closed the door behind him. He had a brown bag filled with left-over biscuits and bits of bacon. He put the treats in his hand and let Mitt eat until he could eat no more. Mitt felt his belly grow round and taut. For a minute he thought that life in town might be sort of nice. But then he looked at his mitten and said, "I think it's time for me to go."

"There's just one problem," said Jack. "Like I said before, if my mother sees you, you're dead, remember?"

Jack paced back and forth thinking about
how to get Mitt and his mitten out of the

house. Then the boy lowered his voice to a whisper and said, "I know, *let's get Digby*."

"Digby? Are you joking?" protested Mitt. The thought of Digby didn't give Mitt much hope. He was big. He was clumsy. And he never seemed to listen. Mitt had no idea how such a dog could get a mouse and a mitten out of the house.

Even so, Jack called for Digby. He arrived on the spot, all legs and tail. Jack placed Mitt upon the dog's neck, and put the ring of Digby's collar into Mitt's paws.

"Now hold on tight, and whatever you do, don't let go until I tell you to," ordered Jack.

The boy put the mitten in Digby's mouth and told him to take Mitt downstairs and into the backyard.

"But what about your mother?" asked Mitt.

"I'll distract her," said Jack.

"How?" asked the mouse.

"Don't you worry. I'm really good at distracting my mother."

Then Jack spoke directly to Digby. "When you get into the yard, sit down by the birdbath and wait for me."

Digby nodded in the way that big dogs do, and Jack patted him on the head.

He opened his bedroom door and Digby went down the stairs without much display. Then, Jack went into the kitchen and poured a glass of milk, spilling it on the floor. As he and his mother were wiping the well-planned spill, Digby went through the back door to the birdbath.

And that's when it happened. A snowshoe hare went racing through the yard. And Digby, giving no thought to sitting by the birdbath, ran off behind it.

The hare, being all legs and light-bodied, was as fast as hares can be. It raced down the street, one block after the next, past the factory and along the riverbanks. Then it turned onto a long dirt road. All the while, Digby was not far behind, bounding left and right while Mitt hung on for dear life.

Running past a barn, Digby dropped the mitten and kept running after the hare. He was gaining on the rabbit when all of a sudden, SPLASH! Digby landed in a huge puddle, stopping him in his tracks. His fur was soaked and his face was so muddy he could not see. And so Digby shook. He shook, and he shook, and would not stop shaking. He shook from the tip of his nose to the top of his tail, and Mitt went flying through the air. Not knowing that Mitt had been tossed beyond sight, Digby saw the hare pop up again and continued the chase. Now Mitt was really lost. And his mitten was gone. Again.

CHAPTER TEN
The Cranes

Mitt had landed in a cornfield. Mitt could tell by the hard stubby stalks and pieces of corn that it had just been harvested. At least he wouldn't be hungry! Mitt filled his cheeks with pieces of dry corn, enjoying every stray kernel. He scooped up the nuggets, sweet and golden, foraging and storing as much as he could. He did not want to be greedy, but did not know how long it would take to find his mitten and get back to the woods.

Mitt was collecting his stash when Gaa-aah—rooooo-ah! Gaaaa-aaah-rooooooo-ahhhh! A strange and eerie sound seemed to be coming from the distance, but Mitt couldn't tell where. Gaa-aah—rooooo-ah! Gaa-aah—rooooo-ah! Gaaaa-aaah-rooooooo-ahhhh!

The greater sandhill cranes were coming in, sailing down on set wings that stretched gracefully from their sides. Upon landing, most milled about quietly on their long skinny legs, poking around the field for bits of food. Right away Mitt noticed one crane more beautiful than the others. She was soft gray with pale white cheeks. Her form was tall and slender yet her back feathers bustled out behind her. Her neck was a gentle curve and the red on her forehead was a soft dull rust color. She looked to be the oldest and wisest, and dancing near her was a large sandhill crane with a really bright red forehead. His name was Blesi, and he was sticking his wings out wide and turning around in circles, tossing tufts of grass everywhere while the others paid no attention to him.

But before Mitt could get out of the field, Blesi stepped right on top of him and pinned him to the ground. Then, unlike the other cranes walking about, Blesi sat down. Everything went dark and Mitt could barely breathe.

It was more than he could take.

"Hey, what do you think you're doing?" yelled Mitt.

But his voice was barely heard from underneath all the feathers.

"Did somebody say something?" asked Blesi.

"I say, *did anybody hear that?*" asked Blesi again.

All the other cranes answered "no," so Blesi didn't think much more about it. But Mitt, on the verge of being squished, had to do something. So he took a blunt piece of thick, dry corn stalk.

Poke! Poke! Poke! He poked at Blesi from underneath.

Gaaaa-roooooo-OW! Blesi popped up and noticed Mitt. In doing so, he drew the attention of the others, and they all circled around the mouse. They peered down at him, eyes gleaming and bills sharp, snapping, and pointed.

Until that moment, Mitt did not fully realize how large a sandhill crane really was. *Up close.*

So Mitt thought of the only thing a little mouse in his spot could do. He said hello.

And the cranes, in the throaty warbled way that cranes do, said hello in return.

Mitt explained about the birthday party and his mitten, Butterball and Digby and Jack, and the hare. He was shivering cold and wet, and had nearly been smothered by a big fat bird. He told them that he wanted to find his mitten and take it back to his place in the woods. Much to his surprise, the cranes understood.

"Which way is home? Which way is home?" the cranes uttered out to Mitt. "We will take you! We will take you!" While the cranes carried on making all sorts of noises, the beautiful crane Mitt spotted earlier walked up and bowed her head to him and said, "Take hold of my wing, little one, and crawl up to my back. I will take you home and we will find your mitten."

Mitt was so happy to find a nice friend, and so did as she said. Once settled, he asked her for her name.

"It is Tuuli," she said.

"Tuuli?" asked Mitt. "What kind of name is that?"

And the beautiful crane answered in a voice that was as soothing as a warm spring breeze. "Tuuli is Swedish for wind."

Tuuli began winging her way along an updraft until she was soaring high above the field, floating on a tailwind, and carrying the mouse toward home.

CHAPTER ELEVEN

Tuuli and Hedda

Mitt told
Tuuli all about the
forest where he lived, and how it was at the
edge of a town called Cheboygan. Tuuli
knew about Mitt's forest. It was Mackinaw
State Forest, and although much of it was
near Lake Huron, there were patches of it
spread in other places throughout northern Michigan. It might not be easy, Tuuli
thought to herself. But Tuuli felt for Mitt

the way she did for her own children, and wanted to bring the little mouse home.

Mitt snuggled into Tuuli's back, watching the Black River below. Tuuli then turned toward Lake Huron, flying over the grassy marshes and wetlands where smaller rivers and ponds attracted groups of resting birds. Tuuli spotted more sandhill cranes and Canada geese. They were gathering together before making their way to Baker Nature Sanctuary in southern Michigan. Tuuli heard them call out to her, but she didn't stop. She told Mitt that she would join them later, after he was home.

Tuuli flew like liquid silver through the gray autumn clouds. Her voice was like a beautiful oboe, pouring out low and delicate tones. Her feathers were supple and warm, and Mitt hadn't felt that type of comfort in a long time. Before long, the near silent whup-whup-whup of her giant wings in flight lulled Mitt into a deep and dreamy sleep.

But as Mitt slept, Blesi and the other cranes appeared, pulling at Tuuli to change course. There was danger ahead! Every year, the birds had followed the same route along the river and wetland, but this year it looked different. There were big machines and noisy diggers scraping at the earth. There were piles of dirt where reeds and shallows and ponds used to be, and men and cars and trucks moving all about. The cranes did not know what this meant, and became nervous in the way that cranes do. Tuuli chose not to wake Mitt for fear he might startle and fall off her back. So she turned with the others, hoping she wouldn't be too far away from his home.

The cranes had no choice but to head further south, crossing the Au Sable River. They flew to Tobico Marsh along the

Saginaw Bay and landed there. Mitt woke
just as Tuuli was setting down and found
the open-water marsh an unfamiliar sight.
He had never seen such a place before, its
cattail edges alive with Caspian terns and
herring gulls and redhead ducks. Tuuli
wanted to tell Mitt how they had flown off
course and would turn around soon.

But there was no time to do such a thing. Hedda, standing like a statue behind Tuuli, was hungry. Tuuli knew Hedda and the two had never been friends. Hedda, the great blue heron, was always in a nasty mood, and before Tuuli could utter a sound, Hedda's bill was coming down upon Mitt's head like a pair of scissors. She had him! Hedda had Mitt in her bill! Tuuli began to push at Hedda when, all of a sudden, a terrible noise broke out of the trees. Kwok! Kwok! Kwok! Out dove five black-crowned night herons, swooping in on Hedda. They poked into her sides, making her drop the mouse. Like Tuuli, the stocky night herons did not like Hedda and were happy for a chance to make her lose her food. But there was no way to thank them, for Tuuli had grabbed Mitt the first chance she could and flew away.

Mitt was happy to be resting in Tuuli's feathers again, and this time stayed awake as they flew onward. Tuuli flew until she came to a field with a stone house nearby, and a pen with many sheep. "We will be safe here, Mitt" said Tuuli. "Tomorrow I will turn around and bring you home."

The tired mouse wiped his eyes. He could not tell if they were filled with sleep or if he was going to cry. Tuuli bedded down in the field, tucking Mitt beneath her as if he were a small, delicate egg in need of warmth.

CHAPTER TWELVE

May's Playmate

Mitt woke to the sound of a horse and wagon rolling down the dirt road. Tuuli was far afield gathering food, so Mitt explored his surroundings. He followed a fence to a batch of metal pails set on the ground. The pails, he noted, were filled with seed. Seed! Mitt was hungry. After Tobico Marsh, he knew he should not leave the watchful eyes of Tuuli, but his stomach got the best of him and he raced to the bucket. And that's when the little girl grabbed him by the tail.

She picked him up and dropped him into the pocket of her pinafore. He heard the cranes garbling and croaking to each other and Tuuli calling out for him. He tried to answer, but his voice wasn't loud enough.

The redheaded girl, whose name was May, hopscotched her way down the dirt road that wound through the grounds at Greenfield Village, where her father worked. There were other items in the pocket besides Mitt. There were two old pennies, a glass marble, and a handful of sunflower seeds. Mitt, still hungry, helped himself to a few bites.

May skipped into the cider mill where her father was putting apples through an apple press. He took bushel after bushel, shaking the contents of each basket into a large machine. He had been making apple cider all day, and the building smelled sweet and warm.

"Daddy, you'll never guess what's in my
pocket," she said.

"Oh, I could take a few guesses, May, but I'm really busy right now. I'm making cider for all the people who will come to Greenfield Village tomorrow."

Mitt listened to them talk to each other. "No, really Daddy, you will never guess, so just try. Please?"

"Ok, May," said her father. "Is it a caterpillar?"

"Nope."

"Is it a piece of peppermint candy?"

"No, again," said May. And before her father could guess again, she grabbed Mitt by the tail and swung him in the air. "It's a mousey!"

"May, be careful," scolded her father. "We can't have a mouse in the cider mill.

We don't want any of the guests to have mouse cider!"

Mitt was thinking almost the same thing. He wouldn't want to be mouse cider. But what could he do now?

The father went on. "May, I want you to take the mouse outside and put it down so it can go back to its home. It probably lives near the Firestone Farm, or in the meadow. It probably has a family like you do. A mother and father with plenty of brothers and sisters."

Mitt's heart sank. He didn't have a mother or father or brothers or sisters. He didn't even know where he was.

When May thought her father was watching, she made a very large motion, *pretending* to grab Mitt and set him free. But instead, she kept him in her pocket. Mitt thought about chewing a hole in her pretty dress and making a run for it. But he had good reason to fear falling into the cider press or getting trampled by a hay wagon. So he had no choice but to speak to the girl, in the way that a trapped mouse will speak.

"Hey, you. You can't do that! Your father said to let me go and you must do as he tells you!" shouted Mitt.

May looked into her pocket, staring at the mouse in disbelief. She peered over her shoulder to see if her father was watching. He wasn't.

She pulled Mitt out of her pocket and set him on the ground, eager to play with him. But before she had the chance, an eastern cottontail rabbit came dashing through, grabbing Mitt in her mouth and whisking him away.

CHAPTER THIRTEEN

Meri the Cottontail

The cottontail was Meri, and she had Mitt firmly in her mouth. Her legs were long and swift, and seemed to barely touch the ground as she made her quiet race through Greenfield Village. Meri loped past old buildings and stone houses to a farm near a patch of oak forest. Once there, she scrambled into a thicket of black huckleberry where her home was cleverly hidden. The thicket was near the barn, and Meri knew the farmer did not like her living so close to his garden. Now safe, the cottontail tucked Mitt into a small, cozy nest where her five cottontail babies were waiting.

Meri had round eyes, set like brown-colored gems upon a buff velvet face. Her nose was pink and twitching, and her ears long and smooth. She greeted her babies by nuzzling them softly, and then told Mitt, in the loving way that cottontails will do, that she was a dear friend of Tuuli's, and Tuuli had once saved her from a red-tailed hawk. She told Mitt that Tuuli had asked her to find him and keep him safe. "Tuuli will return soon," whispered Meri, "Tuuli will return and take you home."

Mitt stayed with Meri and her babies while the autumn landscape changed from brilliant

harvest colors to shades of icy gray. Mitt did not seem to mind, for he was able to leave the thicket every day to forage for white oak seeds and witch hazel. Meri always left at dusk and dawn to feed upon woody sprigs and tree bark, returning nourished and ready to feed her babies again. During this time, Meri treated Mitt as her own, grooming and nuzzling him, and teaching her babies to accept him as a brother. The babies were happy to do so, and as they napped in the nest, Mitt told the baby cottontails stories about his home, and they made soft hushing noises in return.

From the thicket, Mitt watched the first snow fall upon the farmer's field. It made him sad, for seeing the ground turn white made him worry that Tuuli may not return.

One morning, when the trees were dashed with frost, a murder of crows came flying toward the thicket. Meri stood on her hind feet, forepaws tucked to her chest. The crows were cawing and calling, taunting Meri away from her babies. Meri grunted and gave a squeal of worry, warning the crows they were not welcome. But the crows kept at her until she went racing over the field zig-zag, while the crows gave chase.

While Meri was working to lure the crows far away from her babies, Mitt peered out of the thicket. He could no longer see Meri, but could spot the crows diving and dashing at the field, looking smaller and smaller in the distance. Little did Mitt know that on the other side of the field, there was more danger to come.

CHAPTER FOURTEEN
Hiska

The babies were sound asleep and Mitt was nearly too when s*crip, scrip, scrape. Scrip, scrip, scrape.* It sounded as if a thin piece of tin was being scraped along the side of a tree. *Scrip, scrip, scrape.*

The noise startled Mitt, who couldn't tell where it was coming from. Just as Mitt settled back into bed, Mitt saw two eyes peering into the nest. It was Hiska.

Hiska the red fox was well known at the farm. Hiska had waited until his plan with the crows was underway before getting so close to the nest. Now, with Meri far away, it was time for him to snatch the tiny cottontails.

The fox's lips were black and snarling, and his long toenails caught a hint of light as they swiped at the nest. But Mitt was not going to let Hiska snatch Meri's children.

"There is nothing you can do, mouse. Meri is out over the meadow and she won't be back soon. If ever," sneered Hiska.

Mitt would never forgive himself if anything happened to the babies after Meri had been so kind. Mitt secretly tore a solid twig from the black huckleberry and hid it behind his back. He had to think fast. He had to take Hiska off-guard.

Plotting, Mitt said, "I see you like the cottontails, fox. Well, I will give them to you. I will gladly give them to you."

"But first," added Mitt, "you must sit down and listen to a story."

"A story? Why would I want to listen to a story?" snarled Hiska.

"Because," said Mitt, trying to get Hiska to sit down, "if the cottontails wake and scream, as young bunnies will do, the farmer will find us and do away with us all. If you let me tell you a story, because I like telling stories and rarely have the chance to do so, I will let you take them without any fuss. The babies mean nothing to me."

Taking the bluff as Mitt hoped he would, Hiska steadied himself into a sitting position, and Mitt began his tale.

"There was once a sweet maid who needed a shepherd for her sheep. A bear asked for the duty. The young maiden asked him how he would call the sheep and he said 'grr, grr, grr.' The maiden told him no, he would not be helpful calling sheep. Then came the wolf, and when the maiden asked him how he would tend the sheep, he said, 'I will bite their feet.' The maiden sent the wolf away, telling him that would not help a bit. Next came the bobcat, and when the maiden asked how he would tend the sheep, he said he would call them with a 'meow, meow, meow.' The maiden shook her head and walked away, thinking she would never find a shepherd for her sheep."

Mitt watched Hiska with a close eye as he told the story, making sure the fox was listening carefully before he continued.

"Then the maiden met a fox, just like you. The fox begged to be the shepherd, and so the maiden asked him, 'How will you call the sheep?' The fox replied, 'I will cry hey dilly dally! Come to the meadow! And then I will follow them home so they are safe.' The maiden liked his answer, and so hired him on the spot. But the next day, when she arrived at her cottage, her flock had been eaten! The fox had eaten every last one. He had even eaten her oats and her eggs, and cleaned a bowl of cream down to the last drop. The maiden was very angry and took the last drop of cream and threw it at the fox, where it landed on his tail."

At that, Mitt paused to look Hiska in the eyes. The fox was ready for the bait, so Mitt spoke slowly.

"And that is why to this day all foxes have a white tip on their tail."

Hiska, his mouth wide open in disbelief, turned to look at his own tail just as Mitt hoped he would. Right then, Mitt pushed the twig upright between Hiska's upper and lower jaws. It was just the right size, keeping Hiska's mouth ajar so he could do no harm. This drove Hiska wild, and he took off chasing Mitt through the farm. Mitt escaped the fox by scrambling into the barn and hiding in a pile of hay. He had saved the babies and Hiska was gone! But before he could think about how to get back to the nest in the huckleberry thicket, the farmer walked in and pitched the hay into his truck, then got in his seat and drove away.

CHAPTER FIFTEEN
Devil's Soup Bowl

The farmer was delivering hay on his weekly route to Grand Rapids, and when the truck stopped, Mitt was scooped out as fast as he had been scooped in. Mitt was sitting on top of the mound of hay outside

86

a dairy barn trying to get his bearings when he realized he wasn't alone. There were two stowaways in the hay! Their names were Skaldi and Skalli, and they had been riding along with Mitt. They had come from a pond at the outskirts of Detroit and knew the farmer made regular trips with his hay. They were tired of the noise and the cars and wanted to build a new lodge on the Muskegon River, where it was quiet and peaceful.

Skaldi and Skalli knew where they were going, so Mitt, being all by himself, thought he would follow along until he thought of a new plan. But as Mitt scrambled off the hay to begin the journey, he felt something wasn't quite right. *But what?*

The gang of Norway rats had been watching the arrival of the hay. The leader was Borg, and he was as mean as he was big. As

Mitt and Skaldi and Skalli made their way under the fence, Borg and the other rats followed behind. Each had a tail that was naked and long. Each had hairless ears and a large appetite for mice.

Walking along, Mitt told the others about his mitten and quest for home. The forest reminded him of the hollowed out spruce tree, and it made him think about Inger and her birthday party. How it seemed like such a long time ago, he thought.

"Did you say something, Skaldi?"

"Shh. I didn't say anything, Skalli."

"Shh. I hear something," said Skalli.

The animals began to run, hustling through the forest on top of the snow. But soon they came to a spot where they could go no more. It was a large canyon in the

forest. It was not a canyon made of stone, but rather of sand and trees. It was wide and deep, and Mitt could not even see to the bottom. There were broken logs and fallen branches poking through the snow, and as the trio stood at its edge, they heard a dark voice speak from behind.

"It's the Devil's Soup Bowl, you know. Won't you jump on in?"

The rats, showing their full teeth, were standing right behind them.

The three backed up very slowly, until they were at the edge of the bowl.

"My, what do we have here?" asked Borg.

Borg, with one ear half chewed off and most of his tail missing, counted Mitt and Skaldi and Skalli. "One, two, three. I think we have breakfast, lunch, and dinner!"

Borg took a step toward Mitt and scraped his long fingertip underneath the mouse's chin. Mitt stepped backwards, sending him over the edge and rolling into the Devil's Soup Bowl! Mitt tumbled down the slope like a stone, spinning and turning while Borg ran after him.

CHAPTER SIXTEEN
Tuuli's Return

Mitt tumbled down, trying to grasp any root or branch in his path, but he was going much too fast to do so. Borg was only a breath behind when Gaaa-rooooo-aaaaah! Mitt was in the clutches of a bird sailing high up and over the forest. Mitt was dangling by his shoulders when he heard a familiar voice tell him to stay really still. It was Tuuli.

"I said I would bring you home, little one, and I will indeed see that you get home to your mitten."

"Tuuli, what about my friends?" asked Mitt.

Tuuli answered, "There were other cranes along with me, and they will make certain those Norway rats do not bother your friends again. Ever again."

Mitt let out a sigh of relief as they coasted above the snow-crusted fields. They followed the Thornapple River north, watching herds of white-tailed deer browsing on twigs and dry grasses, and wild turkeys scratching and pecking into the snow. Tuuli kept her northerly course until they reached the Grand River, and Mitt watched as it gave way to gentle moon-shaped swales and ponds filled with Canada geese. From the air, they looked like small gray clouds floating upon the water. Mitt was thankful that Tuuli had remembered him and was happy to be heading north.

It was a long trip to Grand Haven along the shores of Lake Michigan. They were following the rolling sand shores near Muskegon when Tuuli began to fly downward. She allowed herself to crest up and over a snowy sand hill before landing among a stand of wild beach grass and sea oats that had turned golden brown for winter. They were a bit north of Muskegon now, and Mitt did not know why Tuuli had stopped.

"Mitt," said Tuuli, "I am going to take you to meet a very special friend of mine. Her name is Elsa and she is a caretaker for the White River Lightstation just up ahead. She will see to it that you get home to northern Michigan—and your mitten."

Mitt did not understand. "Tuuli," he said, "I thought you were going to take me home."

"I am trying," she said, "but I am very tired and the journey this year has proven to me that I am now old and slow. I'm afraid I might not make it and I want to make sure you will. Elsa will get you home, I promise."

With that, Mitt climbed back onto Tuuli's back and bedded into the downy underside of her dense feathered robe. It was here that Mitt felt certain Tuuli wouldn't hear him cry.

CHAPTER SEVENTEEN
Elsa and the Lighthouse

It was not long before Tuuli landed once again. She lit upon a hard-packed sand hill near the lighthouse. Gaa-roo-ahh! Gaa-roo-ahh!

Out came a white-haired woman with a checked wool coat and lantern. It was Elsa, and she was just as Tuuli said. Her face had the soft lines of time, yet her eyes looked as if they held the happy secrets of springtime. Mitt liked her right away but

97

remained at a distance while Elsa put her arms around Tuuli, running her weathered hand along the soft underside of Tuuli's face and neck. Then, Elsa offered her hand to Mitt and said, "So this is the little fellow you told me about! I see what you mean, he is indeed full of character!"

And with that Elsa, Tuuli, and Mitt went inside the lightkeeper's quarters, where they would sleep by the woodstove and eat warm bread and cheese until they could eat no more.

The next morning, Tuuli whispered something into Elsa's ear, and the two of them went outside. Mitt watched as the pair stood at the edge of the cold, snowy shore. Elsa held a wool blanket tightly around her shoulders. Then, without a sound, Tuuli went soaring straight into the icy morning mist that was floating above Lake Michigan. Something wasn't right.

Mitt scrambled out through a broken piece of window caulk and out to Elsa's side.

"Will she come back?" asked Mitt.

"No, she will not come back," answered Elsa.

"Not ever?" asked Mitt.

"Never," said Elsa. Elsa was smiling though her tears told Mitt she was very sad. "Tuuli is old, and she has lived a good life. She has taken care of many young ones."

Mitt, whose heart by now had come to know Tuuli as much of a mother as his own had been, choked back his own tears.

"Tuuli is the Swedish word for wind, you know," said Mitt.

"I know," said the beautiful Elsa with silver-white hair, "I named her."

Mitt and Elsa watched out over the water as Tuuli disappeared beyond sight. The pair walked back to the lighthouse in silence, knowing they would feel sad for a very long time.

CHAPTER EIGHTEEN
The Christmas Gift

Elsa picked up Mitt and placed him in front of the black woodstove. He was cold from being outside and his nose and tail were covered with frost. Elsa stroked him from the top of his head to the tip of tail, singing lullaby songs in a voice that sounded like a lone angel.

That night, Elsa fed Mitt oatcakes with cream and a tiny snatch of grain. She placed a teacup by her bed and let him sleep there, where he would be warm and safe under her watch. If he didn't miss his mitten so much, he may have chosen to stay with Elsa for always.

The next morning was Christmas Eve day, and Elsa told Mitt that in a few days, she would take him to Cheboygan and put him back out in the woods.

Mitt knew he loved Elsa as he had loved Tuuli, and so he wanted to give Elsa a gift for Christmas. A lovely gift so that she'd remember him always. Sneaking outdoors,

he bounded here and there in the snow, trying to find something before Elsa came looking for him. The winter sun was trying to peek through the clouds, but couldn't. The sky was turning dark, and Mitt could tell that heavy snow was coming. Lake Michigan hadn't frozen yet, but there was an icy border at its edge. It was on the border where Mitt saw it. He saw it perfectly.

It was round and shiny and lovely.

And he wanted Elsa to have it.

Mitt drew closer to the button. When he reached it, he couldn't help but sit to admire the pattern on its face. It was growing colder, and the wind was starting to pick up a bit so Mitt thought he better get back to the lighthouse. But before Mitt could turn around with the button in tow, he was blinded by a snow squall.

Mitt clung to the button as the wind came howling through. In an instant, Mitt was blown into the lake.

"Oh no," he cried. "I shall freeze, I shall drown. I will not last a bit in this mess!" Mitt thought it was the end.

CHAPTER NINETEEN
The Ghost Ship

All at once, Mitt heard the quiet sound of wood and wind splitting the water. A lone hand reached down and scooped him up, putting him gently in a basket of sailcloth and ropes. The sailor was wearing a dark blue cap and long coat and had a mustache that went from side to side. He smiled at the mouse as the schooner picked up speed.

"Welcome, my friend. You shall be first mate tonight!" Mitt could not stop shuddering long enough to speak, and the captain, noticing this, took his candle and set it by the mouse. He then placed a wool sweater on top of Mitt and said, "This will warm your sea-worthy soul!"

The smell of the wool sweater and the warm candle made Mitt think about his mitten and how he may not ever see it again.

Mitt began to weep in the low, quiet way that mice will weep when they want no one to hear their sorrow. The captain peeked into the basket and moved the sweater over a notch; just enough to have a real good look at Mitt.

"Say, you almost drowned tonight. What a sad thing that would have been on Christmas Eve."

He picked up Mitt and placed him on his
shoulder. The captain was waving his right
arm from side to side, telling Mitt all about
the Christmas Schooner they were riding.

On the deck, Mitt saw stacks of cut pine and spruce trees, tied in bundles, while one tree stood upright in the center.

"My name is Hermann," the man said. "I have gathered these trees for Christmas. I am taking them to my home in Chicago, so that many families can enjoy them tonight."

Mitt thought the captain was way off course as Chicago was south and they were heading north. He thought the captain might not make it home in time, but thought better than to mention it. He knew how it felt to be lost and far away from home.

The wind whipped through the sails as the captain worked the ropes and wheel to keep his ship steady. The spray from the water made ice upon Mitt's fur.

"Hey little fellow, you look cold." The captain put Mitt in his pocket and brought out a tin box. He opened the lid and brought out slices of hard white cheese and dark brown crackers, and three star-shaped cookies.

"My daughters made the Christmas cookies, would you like a bite?"

Mitt nibbled away, and then drew the courage to speak.

"Do you miss your family?" asked Mitt.

The captain did not seem surprised to hear Mitt speak. He just kept looking ahead as the corners of his mouth lit up with a smile. "Yes, I miss my daughters and my wife very much. But I will be home soon, I know they are waiting for me and I will not be late for Christmas."

Mitt saw that the captain looked as if he might cry. Mitt felt the same way.

The captain steered in closer to shore, trying to find calmer waters in the winter storm. Mitt looked out at the towns lit for Christmas. There were lighthouses and docks, and streetlights with wreaths. As they went further north, the little towns seemed to roll into one long stretch of sand dunes capped with snow, where the hills went high and sweeping up to the sky. It was here the captain spoke again.

"Do you see that large dune right there?" he asked. "That is a great mother bear, waiting for her cubs. They followed her into Lake Michigan long ago, but could not keep up with her. They fell far behind her in the rough waters, and now she is up there—waiting for them."

"Do you think they will make it?" asked Mitt.

"I don't know. Some people say they are still out here, swimming to reach her, but I haven't seen them and I've been out here nearly a hundred years. Mother Bear won't leave that spot until her cubs are with her. She just sleeps there day and night, waiting."

Mitt didn't say a word as he looked at the huge hill in the distance. Although it was dark, the moon cast a glow toward shore, and he could see Mother Bear and her frosty breath escaping from beneath the snow.

And then all of a sudden a thought came to Mitt. I wonder if my mother is waiting somewhere for me? What if she is waiting for me? Could it be?

CHAPTER TWENTY

Old Friends

Mitt had his eyes on Mother Bear when something on deck caught his attention. There were two figures trimming the upright tree. Mitt peered closer. They were wearing fine suits and shaking hands as if they were old friends. The captain stroked Mitt and said, "That's Thomas Edison and

Henry Ford. They arrive every year and decorate the tree for me."

Right then Mitt realized something big. *He was sailing on a ghost ship.*

"You see that lovely lady with white scarf around her neck?" asked the captain. "That's Harriet Quimby, and she's chatting with Rosa Parks." Mitt had heard of Harriet and Rosa, but was surprised to see them out on the schooner. "You see that strong lean kid with the football? That's George Gipp. He plays football for Notre Dame."

Mitt asked, "How did they get here? Have they been here all along?"

The captain didn't answer Mitt's question; he just kept looking out over the water. But then Mitt caught a hint of a silver-pale shadow gliding through the air.

"Tuuli, Tuuli, I'm over here!" Mitt exclaimed. "Tuuli you've found me, you've found me!" Tuuli landed perfectly on deck by the tree, but she didn't seem to hear Mitt calling. Mitt raced toward her. He ran over a pile of ropes and through a mess of buckets.

Mitt kept calling, "It's me! It's me! I see you've come for me!" But Tuuli still didn't answer.

A lone tear welled up in Mitt's eye. Tuuli was so close, yet he couldn't reach her.

Booom! The schooner smashed against a dock at a small fishing village called Naubinway, throwing Mitt to shore. When he landed, he watched the ship vanish before his eyes. The captain was gone. The people were gone. Tuuli was gone. But oh, how nice it had been just to see her one last time on Christmas Eve.

Mitt caught his reflection in the moonlit water. He looked as if he just saw a ghost.

In truth, he had. And now he was all by himself in the Upper Peninsula. Or so he thought.

CHAPTER TWENTY-ONE
Fisk of Naubinway

The night was as
dense as coal.
The pines and cedars
were so thick and snow-laden that Mitt
could not see where to enter the woods.

"Psst. Psst. Over here."

"Excuse me?" said Mitt.

"Psst. Over here, by the bait buckets."

Mitt tip-toed, in the way that frightened mice do, toward a pile of metal buckets stacked near an old brown shack. He saw a dark brown fisher standing over a salmon. The salmon was frozen stiff, and looked as if it had been caught and discarded long ago. The fisher was pushing it around in the snow, but had no interest in eating it.

"The name's Fisk. Who are you?"

Mitt began to answer when Fisk interrupted to say, "Hungry?"

"Yes, I'm hungry," offered Mitt, "but I ..."

Fisk butted in again as Mitt was going to tell him he wasn't much of a meat-eater.

"I can take you into the woods for mouse food, if you like," said Fisk.

Mitt took three steps back. Fishers love to eat mice, so what did he mean, *mouse food*? Did he mean to find him mouse food, *or turn him into mouse food*?

Fisk, seeming to know what Mitt was thinking, said, "Don't worry, kid. It's Christmas Eve."

Mitt softened. He was too tired to be wary. Really, he was quite glad for an escort into the woods. They were dreadfully dark and dense. The night sounds of unknown animals in winter frightened Mitt, so he stayed real close to Fisk until they made it to his den. That night, safe and warm in a burrow lined with grasses and sticks, Mitt told the fisher all about his journey and his quest for home.

By morning, Fisk had decided not to eat Mitt. Instead, he decided to help him.

"I will help you get home. You can follow
me on my hunting trip up to
Tahquamenon Falls. When we get there,
you can follow the river to Whitefish Bay.
From there, hop a freighter and take it to
Cheboygan. Easy as that, kid."

Mitt, leaning in to listen, thought the plan
might work. It wouldn't be easy, but at
least it was a plan.

"What type of freighter?" asked Mitt.

"That part doesn't matter," said the fisher, "coal, stone, boulders, cement, grain."

"Grain?" Mitt's ears perked up a bit.

But Fisk warned, "First we must get to the falls. And when you hunt with me, kid, you have to be fast. And quick. And strong. Like a woodland warrior."

Mitt was no warrior. But what choice did he have?

CHAPTER TWENTY-TWO

North!

Mitt followed Fisk through the woods. It didn't take long for Mitt to be impressed with Fisk. Fisk was fast and could make his way through anything, running along fallen logs and climbing trees branch by branch. Every night, the pair would head north, never far from a stream or frozen riverbed. Mitt followed Fisk as they tunneled beneath winter thickets and ran in between snow-filled branches of the cedar and pine. Fisk was quick and strong, and in time grew fond of Mitt. Whenever Fisk needed to find food for himself, usually a porcupine or snow-shoe hare, he would put Mitt somewhere safe to forage for nuts or seeds.

In return, Mitt grew stronger everyday. When they were tired, they would hole up in a den left empty by another animal, or make a burrow beneath a tangle of fallen trees. Mitt always felt safe with Fisk, and over time the fisher's gruff manner disappeared.

One day, as the pair was going north along the Tahquamenon River in the Lake Superior State Forest, Mitt called out to Fisk.

"Hey Fisk. Did I ever tell you the joke about the skunk?"

"No, you didn't," said Fisk.

"Never mind," said Mitt. "It stinks!" The pair was laughing so hard they didn't notice the trap line in the woods. That is, until it was too late.

It was the first time Mitt had seen Fisk in a fit. The fisher's cheeks pulled upwards to reveal a sharp-toothed grin while his back arched like a mad cat. His tail snapped back and forth while he hissed and growled. He cried to Mitt, "I'm caught, I'm caught! Someone wants my fur coat!" Fisk was snared by his foot and couldn't go any further. The line had tangled him so that he could barely move. But little did they know Mitt was in trouble too. Their commotion had stirred a bald eagle from its nest, and now it was circling Mitt.

Mitt began chewing through the snare, unaware of the bald eagle's threat. Fisk kept thrashing. "Be still," cried Mitt. "You're making it worse for yourself."

All of a sudden Fisk stopped moving. There was an old man standing over him. Mitt sat still too. The pair had no idea what would happen next.

"Hey little fella, what happened?" the old man gently put his broad snowshoe over Fisk's upper body, applying just enough weight to make certain Fisk wouldn't lunge or bite.

"Easy now, let me get you out of here. This isn't how it should go for you today, little fella."

Mitt could tell the man wanted to help, and so moved a bit closer to watch. He could tell his friend Fisk was terrified.

The man noticed Mitt huddling near Fisk.

"How about that! You have a friend, little fella. Ok, there, easy now." Fisk was free, and the man walked away as Mitt and Fisk romped with joy. The eagle had been waiting for its chance to take Mitt, and so when it saw the little mouse dancing unaware, knew it was time.

CHAPTER TWENTY-THREE
Orn

The bald eagle was Orn, and he had Mitt firmly in his thick, yellow talons.

Mitt looked down. That was the last he saw of Fisk.

Orn was not kind, and his intentions were not good. He had hold of Mitt's shoulders, and his talons pinched at his soft round underbelly. Orn kept gliding in circles, each time moving lower and lower toward the pine tree where his gigantic nest was waiting.

Mitt thought it was the end.

He closed his eyes so tight that he didn't even see the pair of Canada geese arrive. They each flew at the eagle, striking it sideways, trying to knock Mitt loose. Who were they and why were they trying to help him?

"We are friends of Tuuli and we are here to help you get home," they honked.

Orn grasped Mitt tighter yet as one goose rammed into his sides once more. The other goose was above the eagle, and Mitt could hear the frup frup frup of her wings beating wildly back and forth.

And then, BAM! The geese rammed Orn once more, and finally, the eagle let go of Mitt.

But now Mitt was spinning, turning, tumbling through the air and down to earth. This was a fall a mouse could never survive.

But one goose moved in to grab him, bringing him downward to a thick, settled marsh. She set him down in a bowl-shaped bed that was hard but not made of wood. It wasn't soft, yet it was warm. It was smooth like stone, yet in many places was thick with velvet. Mitt had no idea where he was, but the whistle of wind through the pines and marsh grasses lulled him into sleep as the goose flew away.

CHAPTER TWENTY-FOUR

Ruben

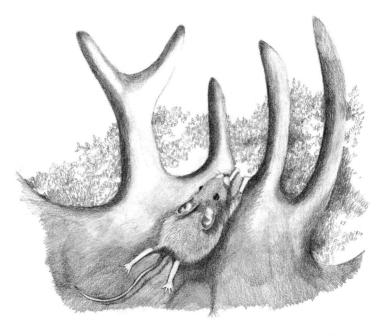

Whoosh! Whoosh! Mitt woke as his bed was being hoisted high into the air. Mitt slid back and forth in the bowl-shaped bed, grasping at the sides, still not knowing what he was sleeping in.

"Whoa!" said Mitt. But before Mitt could jump out, the animal began a full-speed

131

run down a logging road near the swamp.
The way it moved reminded Mitt of Digby,
the Irish wolfhound who galloped along

like a clumsy pony. And like Digby, this animal had skinny legs and knobby knees. But it was dark brown and its head was huge with folds of skin that went this way and that around its neck. It reminded Mitt of the elk back at home, only bigger. *Much bigger*.

When the animal realized it had a guest in its antlers, it stopped. Mitt climbed down and was ready to scamper away when the animal asked, "Who are you?"

"I'm Mitt. But the question is, not who, but what are you?"

"My name is Ruben," said the young bull moose. "I live here." Realizing that the large animal wanted to be friends, Mitt began to tell him of his journey. He told about Fisk and the man, the ghost ship and Tuuli, and his mitten back home. Ruben sat down to listen, much like the way a dog sits down, paying close attention to every word Mitt said. Ruben was big, and he had a tender heart to match his size.

When Mitt finished speaking, Ruben said, "I don't know where my family is, either."

"If you don't know where they are," asked Mitt, "how did you get here?"

"I have heard," said the moose, "that I come from the family that was dropped from the sky."

"Impossible," said Mitt. "Animals are born, they aren't dropped from the sky."

And so Ruben told Mitt the story as it was told to him.

"Long ago, my great-great grandfather lived in Canada. He liked it there, among giant pines and shining lakes. One day, he was snatched by a strange bird. The bird was not made of feathers, but of metal. Its wings were not at its side, but were on its top. It was very loud, and it carried him high into the sky. This bird brought him to Michigan, and dropped him not far from where we stand right now. Great-great grandfather was here for quite some time before the bird came back. When it did, it brought my great-great grandmother."

"But what about your mother?" asked Mitt. "Where is she?"

"One day, my mother left me all alone. I had a lame foot and I stayed by the marsh to rest. She never came back."

"Do you miss her?"

"I do. When I was young, she would teach me how to pull out tender shoots to eat. At night, she would cradle me near her warm chest, where I could hear her heart beat. It sounded like a fist pounding on a deep, ancient drum."

Mitt watched tears well up in the corners of Ruben's large brown eyes. And then the moose said, "When she didn't return, I learned a broken foot will work again, but a broken heart will not."

Mitt liked Ruben very much. Both had deep hearts, and kind ways.

"Ruben," asked Mitt, who was now feeling even more lonesome for his mitten and home in the woods, "do you know how to get me home?"

"No, Mitt, I'm sorry I don't. But I know someone who will. We call her The Tekla, and she lives in the mountains."

Ruben lowered his head to Mitt and the

mouse climbed up between his ears. Mitt took hold of the hair between his brows and settled there.

It was now mid February in the upper peninsula, and the warmer air had made the snow thick, wet, and hard to walk through. The pair stayed in the forests, traveling west for weeks. The journey to Marquette and the Escanaba River State Forest was slow for Ruben, who needed to eat all the time. He would stop to browse on balsam fir. He would gnaw on shrubs and twigs and tall reeds. Ruben was happy to travel with Mitt, and taught him all about how a moose survives in the deep woods. When Ruben's antlers fell off, as antlers will do, Ruben explained to Mitt that it was part of life, and it didn't hurt a bit. All along the way, Ruben told Mitt stories about The Tekla, and how he was certain she would help him find his mitten. It was Mitt's last hope.

CHAPTER TWENTY-FIVE
Spring Arrives

One morning, the forest looked different. The sun was bright and there wasn't as much snow as there used to be. New sounds of birds filled the air, and the trees seemed to be waking from their winter sleep.

The change of season from winter to spring made Mitt realize the passage of time, and so he asked Ruben, in the way that an eager mouse will ask, "When will we get to the mountains?"

"We still have far to go," answered Ruben, "but we can travel easier now that it's spring."

Mitt didn't know anything about mountains. The only thing he knew was that he seemed to be going in the opposite direction of home.

Ruben plodded west with Mitt on his shoulders. There were small lakes and rivers and waterfalls and wetlands, and no shortage of reeds and willows and nuts and shrubs. Once, as Ruben was stumbling through the forest near Laughing Whitefish Falls, he nosed in on a porcupine by mistake. Mitt pulled every quill out with tender care, saving one for a souvenir, weaving it into a patch of thick moose hair behind Ruben's ear for safe keeping.

One night, as Mitt and Ruben were bedding down in the Copper Country State Forest not far from the Sturgeon River, Mitt noticed that Ruben was favoring one foot. Now that it was spring and the sun set later, Ruben had been walking a longer distance each day. Mitt hadn't realized how hard the journey had been for Ruben, and so he stayed awake thinking about how to help him. That's when he heard the dreadful noise.

CHAPTER TWENTY-SIX
Ulf

"What is that?" asked a frightened Mitt. It was a low, long growl that made them both sit up with a start.

"Quiet," said Ruben. "Climb up. We must leave."

But with every step, the pair heard something else take a step too.

But what was it? And what did it want with them?

Ruben ran as fast as he could. He ran due west into the Ottawa National Forest. But no matter how far he ran, the noise followed them. If he would stop, the noise would stop. When he moved on, the noise moved on. This went on for hours before Ruben realized it could only mean one thing, *wolves*.

And he was right. All of a sudden, in a flurry of teeth and growls and fur, the wolves crashed through the understory of young shrubs to close in on Ruben. Mitt held on as the wolves tried to nip the moose from all sides. The leader was Ulf, and he was tall and gray and fast. Mitt thought about Digby, who was tall and gray, but not as fast. And not as mean.

Ulf, in the strong way that wolves do, ordered the others to snap at Ruben from each side while he nipped at Ruben's lame leg. Ulf sneered through his heavy breathing. He knew Ruben could not run fast and was ready to take advantage.

Ruben, not letting up a bit, had a wild, fearful look in his eyes as he smashed through the forest, knocking over saplings and logs and crushing new trilliums and wildflowers in his path. Ruben was fast, but the wolves were faster.

Once the moose was worn down, Ulf spoke. But his words were few. The wolf said, "Ruben, let me tell you about your mother." Ruben thought he knew what this meant. He sat down and let out a bawling sound more sad and lonely than Mitt had ever heard. It made Mitt angry to see how mean the wolf was to Ruben. At that moment, all Mitt knew was that he had to protect his friend. And he needed to do more than tell a joke.

Mitt grabbed the porcupine quill he had been saving and flew off Ruben to face the wolf.

But Ulf started to laugh in the way that wolves will do.

"What's this? A mouse? You think a mouse will save you, Ruben?"

Mitt stood his ground as Ulf stepped closer. And then, as if he were armed with a sword, wham! He stuck the quill deep into Ulf's nose.

But Ulf didn't flinch.

Belloooooo-ow! Belloooooo-ow! The bellowing seemed to be coming from behind them. When they all turned around, there stood

the biggest, darkest moose Mitt or Ruben or the wolves had ever seen. She was ready for battle; her nostrils flaring, her hooves scratching the ground, her head lowered. Her eyes burned with anger as she charged Ulf. Her name was Trind, and she had come to help Ruben.

"Ulf, don't move or I'll undo you myself," said Trind. Then taking no chances, Trind charged full into Ulf, smashing him sideways and sending him and the others cowering away for good.

Trind walked up to Ruben and nuzzled him lovingly. She looked familiar to him, in the natural way that animals remember each other. "Ruben," she said, "when it's time, a mother moose must let her young one go out on its own. I knew it was time for you to do so, and that is why I didn't come back to you. The laws of the forest are not always fair or kind, *but they are what they are.*"

"But I thought you forgot about me," Ruben whinnied softly to her.

"Ruben, I will never forget you. I will always love you. That's why I named you Ruben. *It means son.*"

And then Trind disappeared.

Ruben looked brighter now. His face looked a bit easier. And on that day, his broken foot may not have gotten better, but his broken heart did.

Mitt and Ruben walked slowly now, for the journey had taken its toll. It took them days to reach Nonesuch Falls near the Porcupine Mountains Wilderness Area, where an American black bear had been waiting their arrival. "Welcome," she said. "I was told you were coming. It is time to meet The Tekla."

CHAPTER TWENTY-SEVEN
The Tekla

Mitt and Ruben followed the bear to the edge of the Porcupine Mountains and to the entrance of The Tekla's den.

She was a large and wise wolverine, with a broad bulky body. There were yellowish bands from her shoulders to tail, and her face was small and pointed.

The Tekla invited Mitt into her den and allowed him to get comfortable. The den was hidden below an uprooted tree and lined with leaves and grasses and pieces of fur. The Tekla looked Mitt straight in the eye. And then she spoke.

"You must do one good thing," said The Tekla.

"What is it?" asked Mitt, eager to abide. He had been trying to get home for so long now, he could hardly wait to hear the answer.

"That's it. Do one good thing," she said.

"Do one good thing? Do ONE good thing? But, but ...," Mitt stammered in disbelief. "But you're supposed to tell me how to get home. You're The Tekla!"

Mitt buried his head in his paws. Suddenly,

his anger broke loose like a stone cast into a wasp's nest. "We came all this way so you could help me get home!"

"Yes, you did," said The Tekla, trying to sooth Mitt. "And I will. But first you must do one good thing, and then you will find what you are looking for."

"What one good thing should I do?" demanded Mitt.

The Tekla replied, "I don't know. But when you see it you will know. To all willing hearts, nothing is impossible."

And then she turned away.

Mitt looked at The Tekla as she was walking out of her den. He wasn't sure he liked her. He had come all this way and she told him nothing. *They had made the trip for nothing.*

Mitt was quite hungry, but too tired to forage for food. Ruben was gone. He had left for home. He had such a long way to go, he probably wouldn't even make it home by autumn. How much Ruben had given to bring him to The Tekla, and for what?

Mitt spent three days and nights living in the forest near the ranger station. All that time, he thought about what The Tekla had told him. Ruben had nearly lost his life to bring him here, and he wouldn't have done so if he didn't believe in her. So, perhaps Mitt should believe in her too. Or at least, he should believe in Ruben's belief in her.

Mitt nosed around outside the ranger station, hoping to find some leftover breadcrumbs or camp crackers. The screen door slammed in and out, and with one of the openings, Mitt scrambled in.

He had never been so bold before, but he

was hungry and tired and confused. He was searching the corners for crumbs when a young girl walked in.

"May I hang up this bulletin?" she asked the ranger.

"Let me see," said the ranger, and then he read the paper out loud before hanging it. Mitt listened carefully.

To All Willing:
Heart of Wisconsin Cheese Jamboree
Please Do Come!
One First Prize Cheese Contest
Good Treats and Games
Cheese Smorgasbord, Try
Any Thing You Like!

When the ranger and the girl walked away, Mitt scurried up to the bulletin and read it to himself.

To All Willing:
Heart of Wisconsin Cheese Jamboree
Please **Do** Come!
One First Prize Cheese Contest
Good Treats and Games
Cheese Smorgasbord, Try
Any **Thing** You Like!

To All Willing, Heart of Wisconsin.

Mitt read it over and over again.

To all willing, heart of Wisconsin. All. Willing. Heart. Do One Good Thing. He heard The Tekla's voice again in his mind. *To all willing hearts nothing is impossible. Do one good thing. You will find what you're looking for.*

Right then, Mitt knew what to do. The Tekla said he would find what he was looking for when he did one good thing, and Mitt thought a cheese-eating contest would be a very good thing to do. Then I'll find home, thought Mitt, and my mitten.

With that, Mitt scrambled out the door and began his journey west to the heart of Wisconsin. He had to find the Cheese Jamboree. He had to win the cheese-eating contest.

And so that is how it came to be that Mitt, a white-footed mouse from Michigan, went scurrying into Wisconsin on an early summer day. The red wool mitten had been the only home he had ever known, and now, because he had a willing heart, he had to take a big chance on how to get it back.

COMING SOON...

Minn from Minnesota

Mitten Press is proud to launch this series of chapter books about the adventures of a pair of white-footed mice named Mitt and Minn. In this story, we introduced Mitt in his home state of Michigan. Book Two will present Minn and her life and antics in Minnesota. In Book Three our friend Mitt will venture to a cheese festival in Wisconsin in search of his beloved mitten. You will never guess who he meets there and where their adventures will take them next!

Join Mitt and Minn's Midwest Readers by sending your email address to the publisher at ljohnson@mittenpress.com. You will receive updates as new books in the series are completed and fun activities to challenge what you know about the Midwest states. Be sure to let us know which adventure of Mitt's was your favorite!

www.mittenpress.com

CANADA

LAKE BRONSON
STATE PARK

NORTH DAKOTA

Gra

PORCUPINE
MTN.

M

OTTAWA
NATIONAL
FOREST

MI

Y S
EST
ES
RA

WISCONS

NNE
IOW

ILLINOIS

MONTESSORI LMC
TRAVERSE CITY, MI